Sulwe

For Sekai, the newest star in our night sky
—L. N.

For Lupita
—V. H.

SIMON & SCHUSTER BOOKS FOR YOUNG READERS
An imprint of Simon & Schuster Children's Publishing Division
1230 Avenue of the Americas, New York, New York 10020

For information about special discounts for bulk purchases, please contact Simon & Schuster Special Sales
at 1-866-506-1949 or business@simonandschuster.com.
The Simon & Schuster Speakers Bureau can bring authors to your live event. For more information or to book an event,
contact the Simon & Schuster Speakers Bureau at 1-866-248-3049 or visit our website at www.simonspeakers.com.

Book design by Laurent Linn

The text for this book was set in Young Finesse 9.
The illustrations for this book were rendered using Adobe Photoshop.
Manufactured in China
0719 SCP
First Edition
2 4 6 8 10 9 7 5 3 1
Library of Congress Cataloging-in-Publication Data
Names: Nyong'o, Lupita, author. | Harrison, Vashti illustrator.
Title: Sulwe / Lupita Nyong'o ; illustrated by Vashti Harrison.
Description: First edition. | New York : Simon & Schuster Books for Young Readers, [2019] | Summary:
When five-year-old Sulwe's classmates make fun of her dark skin, she tries lightening herself to no avail,
but her encounter with a shooting star helps her understand there is beauty in every shade.
Identifiers: LCCN 2018029563 (print) | LCCN 2018037928 (eBook) | ISBN 9781534425361 (hardcover) | ISBN 9781534425378 (eBook)
Subjects: | CYAC: Self-acceptance—Fiction. | Blacks—Kenya—Fiction. | Kenya—Fiction. | Stars—Fiction.
Classification: LCC PZ7.1.N96 (eBook) | LCC PZ7.1.N96 Su 2019 (print) | DDC [E]—dc23
LC record available at https://lccn.gov/2018029563

Sulwe

WRITTEN BY
LUPITA NYONG'O

ILLUSTRATED BY
VASHTI HARRISON

SIMON & SCHUSTER BOOKS FOR YOUNG READERS

New York   London   Toronto   Sydney   New Delhi

Sulwe was born the color of midnight.

She looked nothing like her family.
Not even a little, not even at all.

Mama was the color of dawn,

Hardly anyone at school looked like Sulwe either.

People gave her sister, Mich, pet names like "Sunshine" and "Ray" and "Beauty."

Baba the color of dusk,

and Mich, her sister, was the color of high noon.

People gave Sulwe names like "Blackie" and "Darky" and "Night." Sulwe felt hurt every time.

So she hid away while her sister made lots of friends.

Sulwe dreamed of being the same color as her sister.

She wanted real friends too.

So she got the biggest eraser she could find and tried to rub off a layer or two of her darkness.

That hurt!

She crept into Mama's room

and helped herself to her makeup.

Oh no! She would hear about this from Mama.

Sulwe decided to work from the inside out
and ate only the lightest, brightest foods.

With a stomachache, she went to bed
early and turned to God for a miracle.

"Dear Lord,
Why do I look like midnight,
when my mother looks like dawn?
Please make me as fair
as the parents I'm from.
I want to be beautiful,
not just to pretend.
I want to have daylight.
I want to have friends.
If you hear me, my Lord,
and would like to comply,
may I wake up as bright
as the sun in the sky.
Amen."

When Mama came in to wake her for school the next morning, Sulwe rose to find . . . not a trace of daylight in her midnight skin.

Sulwe told Mama everything.

Mama asked, "What is your name?"

"Sulwe," she muttered.

"And what does it mean?"

"Star," Sulwe whispered.

"Brightness is not in your skin, my love. Brightness is just who you are. As for beauty," Mama said, rubbing Sulwe's stomach the way she always did to comfort her. "You *are* beautiful."

Sulwe sighed.

"Well, you are beautiful to me. But you can't rely on what you look like to make you feel beautiful, my sweet. Real beauty comes from your mind and your heart. It begins with how *you see yourself*, not how others *see* you. Now, up you get and out you go."

How could she, as dark as she was, have brightness in her?

How could she have beauty when no one but her mother seemed to see it?

How could she be a star?

That night, a shooting star appeared at Sulwe's window.

"The night sent me," the star said. "Come with me."

Sulwe hopped onto the
star and off they went.

"Long ago, at the beginning of Time," said the star,
"there was Night and Day, and they were sisters."

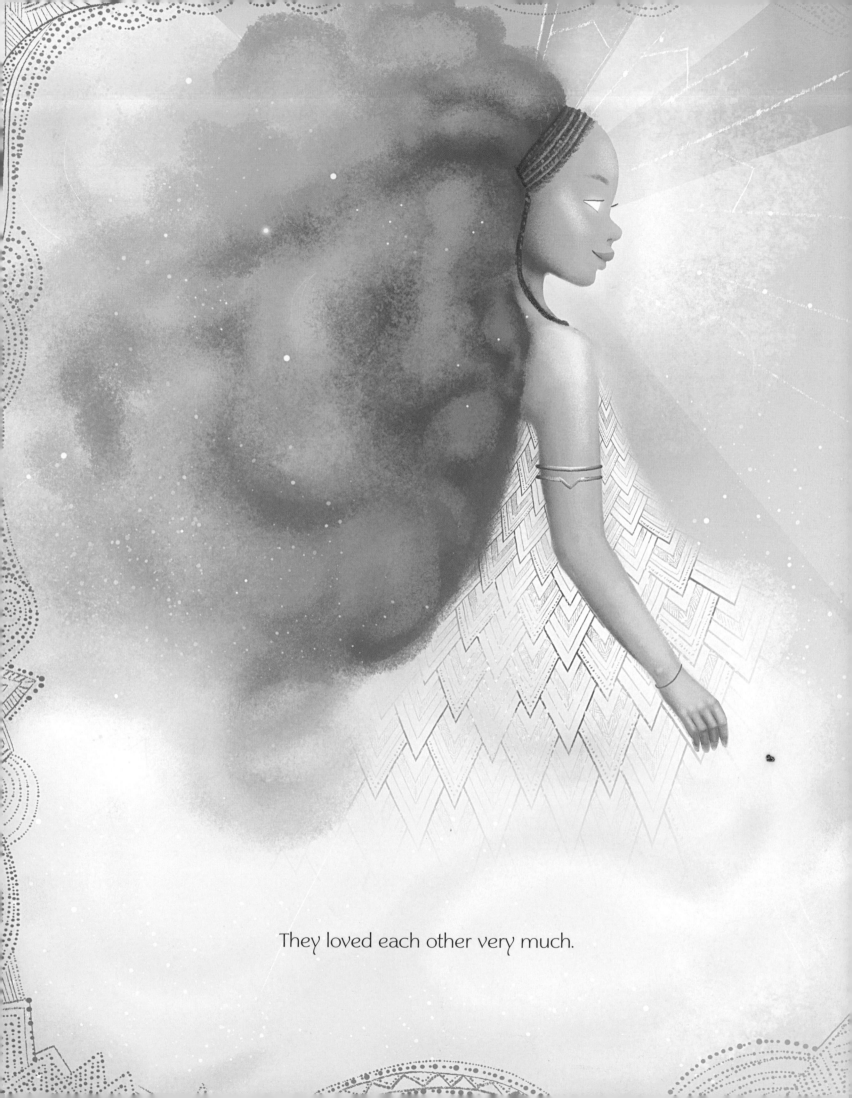

They loved each other very much.

But people didn't treat the sisters the same.

Lovely

Nice

Pretty

People gave Day pet names like "Lovely" and "Nice" and "Pretty."

People gave Night names like "Scary" and "Bad" and "Ugly." She felt hurt every time.

Well, Night got fed up and walked right off the earth.

Scary

Bad

Ugly

Day stayed behind and enjoyed making everybody happy in the sun.

But then Day grew *too* long.

Day began to really miss her sister.
So did everybody else.

There had to be a way to get her back.

Day set off to find Night.

And she did!

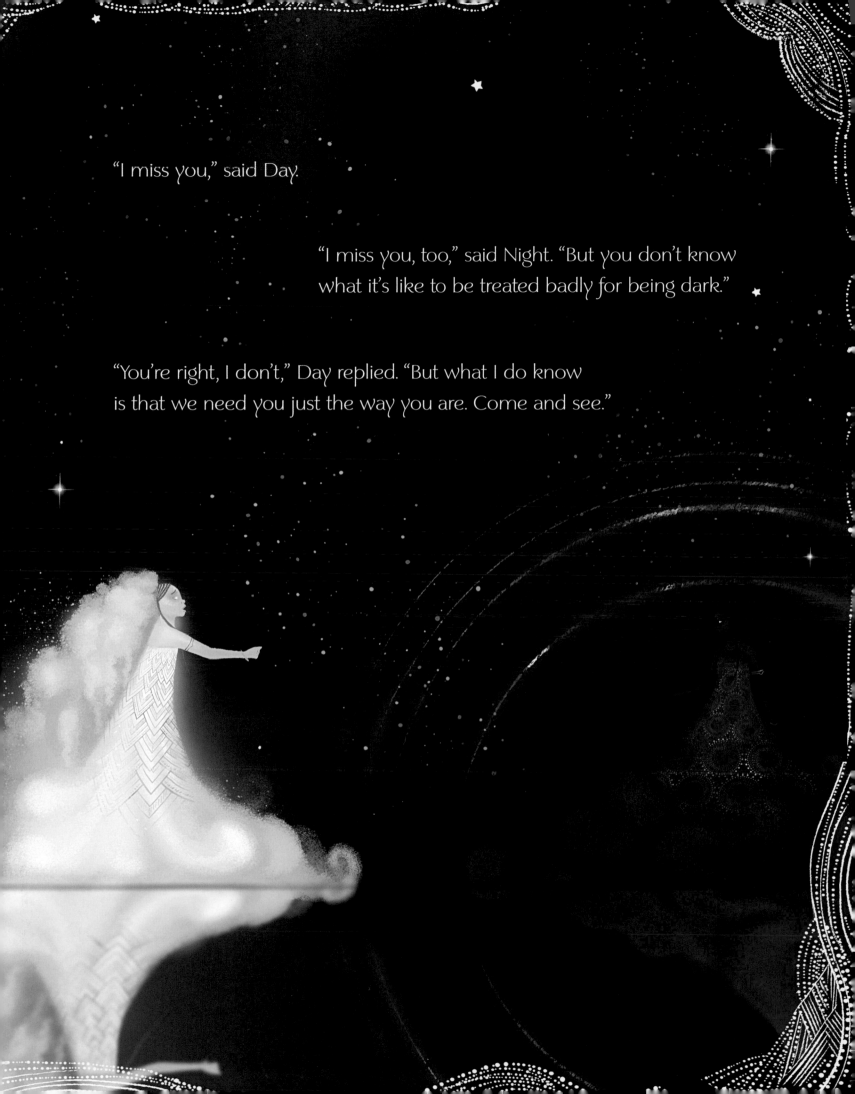

"I miss you," said Day.

"I miss you, too," said Night. "But you don't know what it's like to be treated badly for being dark."

"You're right, I don't," Day replied. "But what I do know is that we need you just the way you are. Come and see."

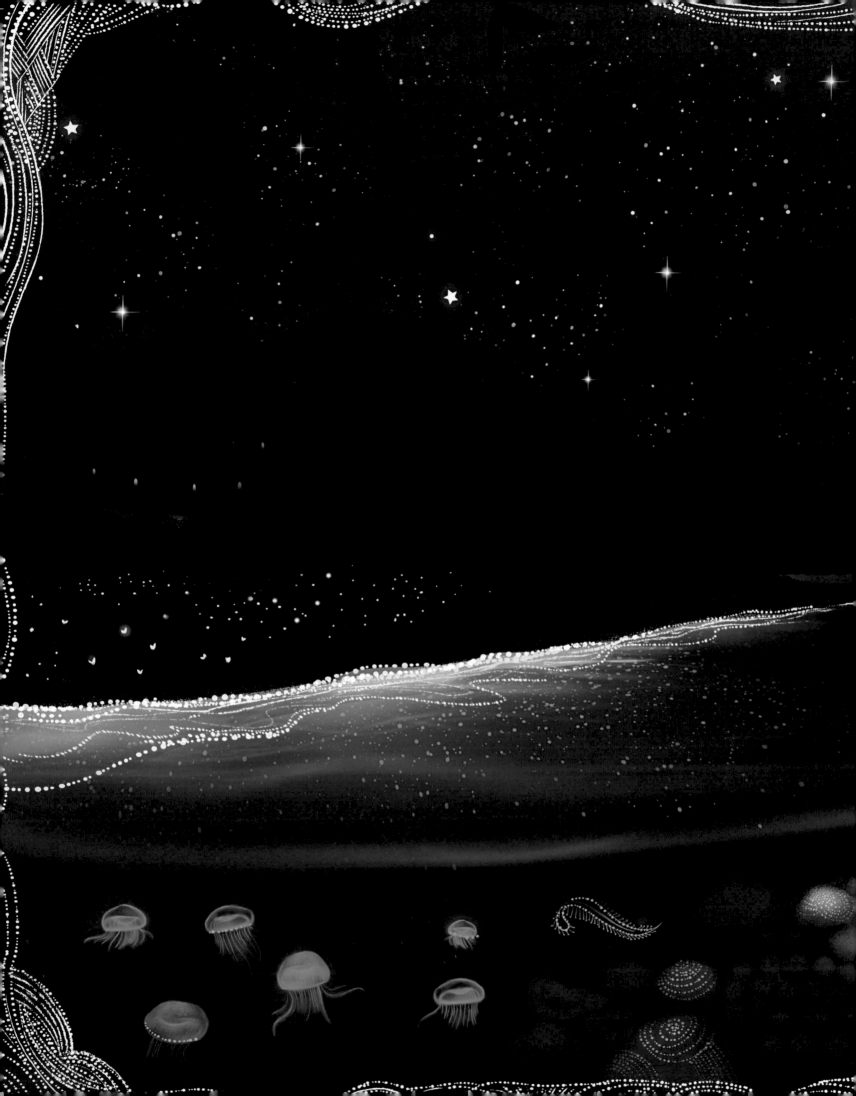

Night returned and the people rejoiced. "We need the darkest night to get the deepest rest. We need you so that we can grow and dream and keep our secrets to ourselves."

The stars chimed in, "Brightness isn't just for daylight. Light comes in all colors. And some light can only be seen in the dark."

While Day had a golden glow, with Night everything had a silver sheen, elegant and fine.

Day told her sister, "When you are darkest is when you are most beautiful. It's when you are most *you*."

Could it be that Night did not need to change, not even a little, not even at all?

Now that Night and Day were back together, a little bit of Night returned to Day in the form of shadows. And a little bit of Day returned to Night in the form of moonlight.

They were inseparable from that moment on, and promised to celebrate the brightness in each other, whether people chose to see it or not.

"You see," the star explained, "we need them both, on their sunniest day and their darkest night, and every shade in between.

"Together they make the world we know, light and dark, strong and beautiful."

Sulwe rose the next morning, beaming.

There would be no hiding anymore. She belonged out in the world! Dark and beautiful, bright and strong.

And if she ever needed a reminder of her brightness, she could look up at the sky on the darkest night to see for herself.

Sulwe felt beautiful inside and out!

AUTHOR'S NOTE

Much like Sulwe, I got teased and taunted about my night-shaded skin. I prayed to God that I would wake up with paler skin. I tried all sorts of things to lighten my complexion. My mother told me often that I was beautiful, but she's my mother, of course she's supposed to think that!

It wasn't until I was much older that my feelings about my skin changed. It helped to see darker-skinned women being celebrated for their beauty. If they were beautiful, I could be too. I began to see myself differently.

While both Sulwe and I had to learn to see our beauty, I hope that more and more children begin their lives knowing that they are beautiful. That they can look to the beauty in the world and know they are a part of it.

And yet what is on the outside is only one part of being beautiful. Yes, it is important to feel good about yourself when you look in the mirror, but what is even more important is working on being beautiful inside. That means being kind to yourself and to others. That is the beauty that truly shines through.

The journey I went on was very different from Sulwe's nighttime adventure, but the lesson was the same: There is so much beauty in this world and inside you that others are not awake to. Don't wait for anyone to tell you what is beautiful. Know that you are beautiful because you choose to be. Know that you always were and always can be. Treasure it and let it light the way in everything you do.

ACKNOWLEDGMENTS

To Mummy and Daddy, who enveloped me
with the unconditional love that led me to my light;

to Simon Green, who saw the glow
and knew I could write this book long before I did;

to Mollie Glick, who tended to the fire
and got me to the finish line;

to Zareen Jaffery, who fanned my flame
and offered the sparks to keep it going;

to Vashti Harrison, who breathed life into Sulwe
and lit the match in her eyes;

to Laurent Linn, whose keen eye trained mine
to tell the fog from the flame, and whose knowing voice fueled mine;

to Ami Boghani, Vernon François, Dede Ayite, Liesl Tommy, Ben Kahn & K'Naan,
who kindled my clarity by saying exactly the right thing
at the right time;

and to *Essence* magazine & Essence Black Women in Hollywood,
who granted me that moment on stage that flared this whole book into existence;

I THANK YOU FROM THE BOTTOM OF MY HEART!